For my family.
For Andrew.

Copyright © 2009 by Katie Cleminson
First published under the title Box of Tricks in Great Britain in 2009 by Jonathan Cape, an imprint
of Random House Children's Books.

Printed in Singapore
First U.S. edition, 2009
1 3 5 7 9 10 8 6 4 2
Library of Congress Cataloging-in-Publication Data on file
ISBN 978-1-4231-2109-1

Visit www.hyperionbooksforchildren.com

handle with care
contains magic

Magic Box

A magical story
by Katie Cleminson

DISNEY · HYPERION BOOKS
New York

On her birthday,
Eva was given a
very special present.

She opened it,
jumped in . . .

For her first trick,
she wished for
what she most
wanted in the
whole world:
a pet called
Monty.

Monty turned out to be rather large.

For her next trick,

Eva pulled rabbits out of hats.

Then, with a flick of her wand,

she made things float in the air.

For her biggest trick of all, Eva threw a huge party.

There was lots of

delicious food,

the very best musicians

and
plenty
of
dancing.

When everyone had danced their socks off,

Eva
shut her eyes,
clicked her
fingers . . .

and everything vanished. . . .

Well,
not quite
everything.